I've Finally Found You, Now What?

Dr. Henry Bernard Miller

India T. Miller

"Now That I've Found You"

Copyright 2019 by Henry Bernard Miller

Printed in the United States of America

Acknowledgement

First, I give thanks to God for all He has done in our lives. This project could not have been done without His guidance and His Strength. Also, I want to thank all who in one way or another contributed in the completion of this work. I thank my family and friends for their encouragement. Finally, I thank my wife India for allowing me to talk about us.

Table of Contents

Foreword

I am indeed honored and count it a privilege to have been invited to give contribution to such a love story written so eloquently from the heart and honest place of the authors' Dr. Henry Bernard Miller and India Miller.

Dr. Miller is a profound and prolific teacher. He has conducted and taught many through seminars and workshops throughout the country. India Millers' contribution to the book allows other women to understand themselves and gives them hope as women that one failed relationship does not define your destiny, but allows God to bless you with the mate intended just for you.

The authors' ultimate goal in writing the book is that others will be able to take away tips and pointers that will enhance and give a whole new outlook and meaning to new found love through the eyes of God. The authors' work gives clear meaning to the word "mate" as God sees it.

There are tips in the book, as it pertains to understanding, listening and forgiveness that will be conducive to any relationship from the beginning to the end. Relationships are, by no means, easy but it takes everything to make it work. It's not controlled by "feelings" or "emotions" but it is a choice as the author stated. Making God the center of any relationship will always amount to a "win-win".

Follow the blueprint in the book, inspired by God, and bask in the blossoming of your relationship for years to come.

Lynn Brown

Co-Author Next Level Shift Vol II

Introduction

How do you find a new relationship? Whether you've been single for years or are only recently on the market, seeking out a compatible partner is not always easy. It was not easy for me. I had friends that I went out and socialized with on occasions. These relationships never blossomed into anything serious. I didn't like the idea of leaving casualties. I must say that over the years I have been graced with some wonderful ladies in my life. One researcher said that dating prepares you for your real mate. So, as you date, keep that in mind and don't give away something that might end up belonging to someone else (If you know what I mean).

I have concluded that finding love is a walk of faith. It is my prayer that as you read this book you will get a few pointers to help along the way. This reading also can be a helpful guide to your current relationships. Consider the following points before setting out to find a partner. There are no guarantees in love, but a good start might help you move in the right direction.

Do you know what you want? Are you looking for a hook-up or a spouse? Be honest with yourself and find ways to be consistent with your relationship goals. I was a little different because I've never wanted just the hook-up. There was always a chance that you might hook to the wrong wagon. So, I kept asking myself questions.

Are you really prepared to invest the needed time?

Do you know your value as a potential partner?

Have you given yourself a chance to grow?

So, I made finding my mate a priority. Since I didn't have a clue on how to do it, I was left depending on my faith. I am so thankful for this journey. I pray that you will use this information to help make your story. Finally, your mate is out there waiting. You may have to go through some things to find them. They may be going through some things while waiting on you. Keep trusting God that your journeys will meet.

Dr. Henry Bernard Miller

1

Now That I've Found You.

After several years of looking, I've finally found her. Now What?. I must admit that the fear of past failures were on my mind. I didn't want to mess up what I thought was a God given opportunity. The pursuit started with me inquiring about this young lady singing on the Praise Team of a local church. When I saw her, I have to say, I was singing Johnny Gill's song, "My, My, My, My, My, My, My, Sho Look Good Tonight. You are So (bleep) fine." You all know the song and the words. She was singing the Lord's songs and didn't know I was stalking her church's Facebook page. That continued for a few months. I finally asked a friend to let her know that I was interested. This was so different for me. The friend shared with her my interest. Well, no response. I backed off and continued enjoying the praise team on Sunday Mornings. Until one evening while strolling through Facebook. She had posted that she had gone to the movies alone. So, I responded and inquired about her outing. To my surprise, a conversation started. Eventually, the conversations moved into some deep life discussions. Those late night messages on messenger became the normal thing to do. Between typing slow and going to sleep, I managed to keep up. April 5th 2019, the discussion was getting a little too deep for messaging. So, I popped the question, "why don't we meet at Red Lobster in a 1hr and a half." I was not expecting her answer. She agreed to meet me. Just for your information. She had never heard my voice. I didn't have her cell number. Didn't know much of anything. All our communication had been done on messenger. The only thing that mattered to me was that I finally get to see her face to face. When I walked in the Red Lobster we gave the normal greetings. She was even more beautiful than I expected. I found out that her beauty went deeper than the exterior surface. After sitting for about five minutes, she began to cry. I was startled for a moment because we were sitting in this public restaurant. I didn't want people to think that I had done anything to her. She bore her soul to me. I heard and felt her pain. It was at that time that I realized this woman was my wife. God spoke to my heart and said, "If you want her, you must build her up." Ever since that day I've tried to be a brick mason.

What those who have found true love know is that it is not an experience of total fulfillment or enchanted whimsy (and feeling that way doesn't necessarily mean its true love, either). True love is actually about meeting another person in their purest form, and cherishing what you find. It's not something you discover by chance or fate, but something you cultivate. It's one of the greatest tools we have to reach our deepest selves, and to share the joy of what we find.

Through all of this I've found 9 things about finding love.

1. You are equals. This is simultaneously the simplest and most difficult thing to learn. Oftentimes one partner either sacrifices or demands more from the other. When this imbalance persists, it leads to resentment on one end, and a sense of entitlement on the other. True-lovers realize that their feelings and needs are no greater, and no less, than the others.

2. You're not lovers and you're definitely not best friends. You are family. So often we hear that the most successful relationships started out as friendships. I was a true believer in this concept. But true-lovers know that their bond surpasses any friendship they could ever have, and that their physical intimacy as lovers is inextricably

tied to it. They're family because their connection runs deeper than loving each other and liking each other, than making love and laughing. They are life fixtures that could never be replaced.

3. It's not about how much you laugh together, but how much you cry together. (I promise I didn't get this from a fortune cookie.) True-lovers are willing to be vulnerable together. They're beyond the "I can't let you see me cry or think I'm weak," mindset, and that openness to each other's vulnerability is far more precious than anything else they share.

4. When you have 'problems,' you recognize it's not something wrong between the two of you, but dissatisfaction inside yourself (or inside each of you separately) that interacts. Many relationships end when a set of problems just won't go away, when partners aren't willing (or even able) to adjust to the other's needs. True-lovers know that the problem isn't in their partners, but in themselves. Your needs and feelings are responses to the pain inside of you that's seeking healing or recognition from your partner. True-lovers consider what inside makes them feel the way they do, and if their own demands are causing their partner reciprocal feelings of hurt or inadequacy. They accept their responsibility, which is the ground for forgiveness.

5. Communication actually is key, but only if it's honest. Openly discussing your insecurities, past traumas, and little daily hurts allows your partner to really glimpse into your heart, and have an appreciation and respect for what they see there. Likewise, resentment is the root of all evil. When communication ebbs away, or holds back parts of the truth, annoyances build up inside and resentment is born. True-lovers know this is the wedge that is most difficult to unstick, so better to never allow it to form.

6. You cannot change the other, and you would never try to. So many people think they can change their partners, to mold them into the image of perfection they've imagined. True-lovers never do this, because what they love is their partner exactly as they are. Yes, there are flaws and frustrations (opportunities to grow together), but those things only add to the other's humanness. Demanding that perfection is again a projection of the perfectness you wish was within yourself.

7. Things will change. Staying together is a choice, and it has nothing to do with romance or destiny. Romance is what we see in the movies, when the man runs in and proclaims the woman is his soul-mate and he could never be without her. That is not true love. True-lovers recognize that they will change, situations will change, and their love will wax and wane, maybe even day to day. They know that staying together is a choice, and not predicated on falling in and out of that romantic, fated idea of love.

8. Your partner could never complete you, and expecting them to is not only selfish, but toxic. Again, cultural romantic thinking. Completion is internal. It's painful, delicate work inside your own soul. To expect it from another will be the thing that destroys the beauty in what you have. It puts a weight on them they could never carry, nor fulfill. True-lovers know they don't need each other, but their love brings them meaning and companionship in the present moment.

9. Nothing could ever break you up. Not because your love transcends all things, but because you recognize your lover's true humanity. You accept the good and the bad, and when one side is more in play, it doesn't make you forget the existence of the other.

This is most important of all in discovering what true love is. True-lovers understand that everybody incorporates the duality of good and bad, because love, in particular, draws out the most extreme in both sides. When you have true love, you've seen your lover in their worst form. When you come to know someone wholly, and accept their humanity as both special and flawed (and you still love them), then pretty much nothing could pull you apart.

2

Be There

Being there is very important. This is a valuable component to any relationship. You must be present and accounted. Love doesn't grow and flourish because you dress up or make yourself up. All it needs is for you to show up, to be fully present.

I used to believe soul mates were mythical creatures, as rare as unicorns, and that finding your soul mate was an honest to goodness miracle—one that happened to other people.

Not true.

Someone is ready to love you. They're out there. And they're looking for you right now. But you have to show up fully to connect with them.

In the past, I spent a lot of time caught up in my head, paralyzed by my fears and insecurities. When I was focusing all my energy on protecting myself, I wasn't available to the people around me. You can't love or be loved when you're physically there but mentally somewhere else.

I now know that I need to focus more on the person in front of me than my worries, insecurities, and judgments. Love can only unfold when you get out of your head and get into your heart.

When you love someone, the best thing you can offer is your presence. For many years I allowed ministry to consume the majority of my time. It eventually cost me my family. Please know that it is important to be there. All the non-essentials can wait.

3

Be open.

Love is a powerful force, but you can't share it if your heart is closed.

I used to fear the slightest puncture in my protective force field. I worried that if I opened up even a little, it would be the end of me. Somehow staying closed felt like protection. If I let someone in, I couldn't control what would happen. If I kept everyone out, nothing could go wrong.

But I learned that you don't need to expose the deepest parts of yourself all at once to be open to love. You just need to let your defenses down long enough to let someone else in.

I started by sharing a little about myself—my opinions, my feelings, and my worries. A little at first, I tested others' reactions to what I shared. But my confidence grew much more quickly than I expected. And you know, not holding back so hard or pretending turned out to be the biggest relief ever.

"The greatest asset you could own, is an open heart."

6 Ways To Be More Open With Your Partner

Relationships are never easy. They take a lot of work, but if you push through all the hardships and turmoils, then you can find ways to emotionally communicate better with your partner. Relationships are about creating a life with another person. Unlike family, you choose to have that person in your life because you deeply love and care for them.

Both of you have been through thick and thin and you pride yourself in the respect you have for one another.

Relationships take a lot of hard work to make them work. I don't think I have ever heard of a perfect relationship, and if you have, well that person is probably lying. Everyone has a few key qualifications that they need to have in a relationship. For some, honesty trumps loyalty, while for others, sex is above being wealthy. Even though, all of these are pretty important to have in a marriage, I believe communication, especially open communication, is a huge factor in making a relationship truly work. If you and your partner know how to communicate with each other, then you have a pretty solid relationship. It's a great feeling knowing you can go to your partner with any concern or thought and know they are going to respect and empathize with you. But being completely transparent with your partner is not everyone's strong suit. It will take practice and determination to get it just right. With a few tips below, you and your partner will be communicating well in no time.

1. Ignore Your Fear of Rejection

When it comes to being open, you have to let go of the thought of possibly being rejected. Being open means being vulnerable, and for you to achieve an honest and open relationship, you can't be afraid of what the outcome might be. If you can't be open with the person that you love because you are afraid of what they might think or say, then that is not a relationship to be in. Your significant other needs to be empathic and understanding when you are expressing your feelings, because it's not easy for everyone to be verbal about how they feel inside. Take baby steps when it comes to being open with your partner. If they are not reacting in a positive way, explain to them how that makes you feel. It could help them understand where you are coming from.

2. Be Honest

Don't be afraid to be completely honest with your partner. I'm not saying make-them-cry honest, I just mean to be honest with your feelings and don't lie to make them feel better when it comes to serious conversations. You are doing more harm than good. I appreciate it when my significant other can be vulnerable and honest with me. I feel it makes us closer as a couple, which then makes me feel like I can be open and honest with her. We are going to discuss honesty more in the next chapter.

3. Say Statements, Not Questions

Don't try to beat around the bush when it comes to your emotions. Sometimes people ask questions instead of saying statements as a passive aggressive way of looking for an answer they want. Instead, just be honest with yourself by saying exactly what you want in an "I" statement way and not a "you" statement. This will help clarify any misinterpreted feelings and allow you and your significant other to get straight to the point.

4. Align Your Feelings with Your Behavior

Try to think about how you are feeling inside. When you become emotionally intelligent with yourself, then you are able to figure out how you can relate that to your outside behavior. Don't try to hide how you really feel. You are not being fair to your mate nor yourself.

5. Explain What You Want

Don't be afraid to be direct. It's a key way for you and your significant other to be understanding of certain things and how they affect you. When you explain what you want, whether it pertains to the relationship or some outside influence, there really should be no room for confusion.

6. Have Open Dialogue

Essentially, you want to stop using one worded answers. It's hard for some people to be open when all they are receiving is a "yup" or a "no" answer in a conversation. While single phrases are direct, they don't really explain a lot. And that is the whole point of being more open with your emotions.

You have to explain yourself, be vulnerable, and not be afraid to be open. I want our relationship to always be open with feedback and dialogue. Communication is key in any relationship, but if one person is doing most of the emotional talking, then it might just be a one-sided relationship, and that doesn't benefit anyone.

Being open and vulnerable can be a scary thing. But it's better to do so than to start being resentful and regret not doing it in the first place. With these key tips, you will be on your way to a very emotionally stable relationship.

4

Be Honest

Being truthful in love goes further than just not telling lies. It takes being the real you, the wonderfully imperfect you.

Pretending to be someone you're not or disguising how you feel sends a worrying message to the person who loves you. Human beings have an inbuilt alarm when they sense someone isn't telling them the whole truth.

I had an image of the 'perfect me,' and it didn't include being vulnerable. So I lied about the true me in everything I said and did. I pretended that I didn't worry, didn't need help, and that I knew exactly where I was heading in life. Those lies alone alienated some amazingly wonderful and loving people who would have been life-long friends... if I'd let them.

Here are 5 things that happen when you're in an honest relationship:

1. You grow spiritually and emotionally.

When you are in an honest relationship, you learn things about yourself through your counterpart. You grow together in many aspects. You enrich each other. No one is pushing anyone. You are both gently expanding and changing to the best parts of yourself. An honest union enhances each other to grow. They support one another in careers, parenthood, spirituality, health, sexuality, and other facets of life. As individuals you thrive, and together you are a team.

2. You are vulnerable, and it's freeing.

Trust is underrated in relationships. It's that one component that binds partnerships. Once that's gone, it's difficult to get it back. Vulnerability is perhaps the glue that holds an honest union together. It takes courage and strength to be raw. By exposing all to one another, you are set free of expectations, assumptions, and disappointments. There are no guessing games. There is no hidden agenda. You can show the strong and weak parts and still be loved by your mate.

In an honest relationship, there is no criticism because you are both open to whatever happens. This becomes part of the attraction. It's not based on co-dependency, but rather the admiration of strength and courage. At times, life is a journey of challenges and difficult circumstances, but together you make it through.

3. You forgive easily.

There are no perfect relationships, because we are imperfect humans. We will make mistakes. We will have bad days. You will argue and disagree on many things, however you don't hold grudges. You get past it and move to the next issue. You learn that holding anger is destructive, so you move away from it by letting things go. Forgiveness solidifies the partnership. You learn the art of agreeing to disagree while still supporting the other. As Martin Luther King Jr. quoted, "Forgiveness is not an occasional act, it is a constant attitude."

4. Your self-worth is in a healthy place.

You can both admit your weaknesses and still love one another without judgment. A healthy sense of self-esteem endows us with the ability to give. To the degree that we do not like ourselves, we cannot receive, we can only take. The more self-esteem we have, the more we are whole, as receiving is a natural consequence of giving."

When we are in an honest relationship, we feel good about ourselves. We can transform and transcend love for ourselves because we are being emotionally sustained.

5. You learn to cooperate, compromise and communicate.

In this new era of self-promotion, it seems that communication is not always available. Most people put themselves out there in social media without any regard to their partner's feelings. But, healthy-loving relationships understand and accommodate each other. They affirm one another to meet their needs. Compromising is healthy, but it can also lead to unhealthy boundaries where one partner is constantly taking and the other is always giving. Cooperation is a unit and you learn to faithfully support one another. But without communication, there is nothing.

The key to an honest relationship consists of the 3C's: cooperation, compromising, and communication. Honest relationships don't take the other person for granted. They don't bulldoze one another. They know that in order to succeed in their partnership, there is equal parts of giving and receiving. There are times that they will need one to help pull the other up. Communication allows them to freely share without feeling used or abused.

Honest and loving relationships learn from each other. They learn new perspectives, share goals, and succeed because they are a team. They grow through the changes. They compromise, share, support and most of all, provide a safe haven for their souls to transcend.

There is nothing more beautiful than the authenticity from your partner who is also your best friend.

"Honesty is more than not lying. It is truth telling, truth speaking, truth living, and truth loving." ~James E. Faust

5

Be kind

I wasn't kind in the beginning. I was too insecure to let the little things go. A forgotten request felt like rejection. A different opinion felt like an argument. I was also too insecure to accept that it didn't mean I was loved less.

Being kind in love means accepting that people can't always meet your expectations, and giving the other person leeway in how they act and respond. It means looking after the other person's heart even when you're disappointed.

12 Ways to be Kind and Loving in a Relationship

The presence of love and kindness in a relationship can promise a happy and fulfilled life with your partner. Without these two qualities, anger, bitterness, and resentment can easily dominate a relationship that can end with a heartbreaking ending.

Love and kindness come in many forms, and while words are often used to express them, there is nothing more meaningful and genuine than actions and gestures – no matter how small or simple they are.

Here are some of the ways to be kind and loving in a relationship that can help you become a better partner.

1. Be their peace of mind.

Show your love and kindness by being their peace of mind. Life can be messy and chaotic sometimes, and we often find ourselves lost and confused. That is why, it's important to find a refuge where we can feel safe, a peaceful place where we can just breathe.

2. Love them sincerely and genuinely.

Love expressed out of sincerity and genuine care is the greatest love there is. While some people claim to love another just because they make an effort to be with them, true love is actually more than your willingness to be physically connected to another person.

True and genuine love is beyond the physical and is characterized by acts of selflessness, concern for another person's well-being, and the feelings of contentment that come from just seeing that person happy.

3.   Be a source of comfort.

Be a source of comfort in the world full of uncertainties, not only for the person you love but also for everyone around you. Loving someone means giving them a shoulder to cry on, a refuge to run to whenever life becomes too much to bear.

4. Choose to be kind than to be angry.

People make mistakes and most of the time, our initial reaction is to be angry and to do something that will hurt them back – but if you truly love a person, why would you choose anger over kindness?

Learn to forgive and be kind especially if your partner did not mean to hurt you.

5. Respect and appreciate others.

Learn to respect and appreciate other people, especially your significant other. If you want someone to feel that you love them, appreciating and recognizing their existence in your life as a friend, a lover and a life partner, can be the most fulfilling gestures that you can practice.

6. Lend them your strength.

Loving someone means giving them the strength to face life and fight for what they love. Lend them your strength and share the burden with them. Make them feel that no matter how weak they think they are, they can also overcome these obstacles because you will be there.

7. Show them the beauty of living.

Loving someone means helping them to appreciate the beauty of life and living – especially when it matters the most. When times are tough, remind them that life can still be beautiful. When things aren't going their way, help them remember that these are just challenges designed to help them grow.

8. Inspire them to be more positive.

Loving someone means helping them see the brighter side of love. When someone you love complain a lot about their daily struggles, absorbing these negative emotions and feeling equally frustrated can do more harm than good. Instead of sharing the burdens of these negativities, teach them how to be more positive.

9. Treasure every moment you have together.

Showing your love to your partner involves celebrating memorable moments together, treasuring every piece of those memories and keeping them in your heart. A relationship doesn't always have to be about romantic dinners, travel dates or even movie marathons – it can also be about conversations, talking in your love language, or just "good morning" texts. In fact, it's the small things that matter.

10. Make faith the center of your relationship.

The ultimate way to be kind and loving in a relationship is to recognize faith as the center of your commitment. Your faith and your beliefs will remind you that your purpose as a person is to spread love and kindness, not just to your significant other but to everyone around you.

Becoming a better person for others can help you become the best person for yourself – and it's this goal that will help you achieve true and genuine happiness.

11. Teach them self-love and self-care.

Remind your partner to love himself/herself first before trying to give love to others. This is because, if you want to truly love someone, you have to make sure that you have enough love to give – but this is only possible if your happiness does not depend on other people.

Most importantly, make sure that you don't give all your love to someone by leaving some for yourself. Most of the time, people tend to forget this part of being in a relationship and when it doesn't work out, they are left with nothing.

12. Choose your words well.

Words can be powerful. A single line can change someone's life just as how a single word can tear it apart. Practice kindness by choosing your words well, especially during the times when you feel angry, betrayed or hurt because these are the moments where words are like sharp daggers that can easily pierce one's heart.

Be kind and be calm when dealing with these challenging moments because the consequences of your actions after a temporary argument can have lasting effects in the future. Love your mate enough to always choose to be kind even if the circumstance demands you to choose hate.

Love and kindness teach people to love life, especially for couples in a romantic relationship, despite the challenges that they face every day. In fact, these two qualities serve as their source of hope and strength whenever they think that their only option is to give up.

Being a kind and loving mate will not only help your relationship to grow, but it can also make you better people not just for each other but for everyone around

"Be kind whenever possible. It is always possible." ~Dalai Lama

5

Be willing to listen.

Love needs to be heard to flourish, that's pretty obvious.

Love is a conversation, not a monologue.

Because you can't speak the language of love until you learn to listen first.

5 Ways to Be a Good Listener

Opening your heart to your mate—and nurturing theirs—requires listening well. With so many different issues, obligations, devices, and people pulling at us from every direction, it can be difficult to slow down and truly listen to one another. Listening can be pleasant, but sometimes it's downright hard. Sometimes, you might want to tune out and lose yourself in your favorite pastime

Instead—or dive into the list of to-do items you still need to cross off before the day is over.

But to have a healthy, thriving marriage, it's critical to truly listen to your mate with empathy and generosity. Let's look at five ways you can be a good listener for your mate.

1. Listen with empathy

When you practice empathy, you're putting yourself in your mate's shoes and seeing things through their eyes. Whether you're trying to resolve a conflict or just simply listening to your spouse talk about their day, it's beneficial to both of you to listen with empathy when your spouse speaks to you. For you, it gives you a window into their world and their perspective. For your mate, knowing that you're listening from an empathic vantage point helps them feel secure.

Maybe your mate needs to vent about work, and normally, you tune out when they start talking about their tough day or their challenging project. Instead of switching your mind off while they talk, try to see the events of the day through their eyes, and in the context of your life. Have you been dealing with problems at home, like financial issues, trouble with the kids, or taking care of an ailing parent? Contextualizing your whole life along with what's happening at your mate's job will help you understand the level of pile-on they're dealing with.

2. Listen for emotion

When your mate needs to talk to you about something—especially if it's something hard—it's easy to get wrapped up and carried away by your own emotions on the topic. In that case, you might respond to your spouse in a totally inappropriate way in your attempt to alleviate the difficult emotions that come up for you. Instead, take a minute to listen for what your spouse might be feeling. This type of intentional listening goes hand-in-hand with empathy.

Once you've identified what your mate is feeling—whether it's anger, sadness, frustration, anxiety, or excitement—you can adjust your responses based on their emotional state. It gives you an extra chance to check yourself before you say or do something that might exacerbate the emotional state they're in. When our emotions go into a tailspin, it can be difficult to keep communication healthy.

3. Listen without bias

You've both got your opinions, and it's hard to let those opinions go in favor of simply listening to one another. Listening without bias is helpful when you have opposite stances on certain issues, or when you're locked in a stalemate during a fight. Set your opinions aside for long enough to hear what your spouse is saying, then practice your empathy skills to try to understand why.

This doesn't mean you have to change your opinion to match your mate's. What it does mean is that your mate deserves to be heard, and you can't truly hear if you're filtering everything they say through your own bias.

4. Listen lovingly

When you're communicating with your mate, it can be helpful to use loving gestures and body language to let them know you care about what they have to say. It can be as simple as holding eye contact and nodding to affirm what they're telling you. You could also reach out to touch them or hold hands. Turn your body toward them, or even stop what you're doing and just sit with them if that's what they need.

While you may be able to go about your business and have a conversation at the same time (and that can be okay sometimes), there are going to be times where you need to just put everything down and focus all your attention on your mate. Turn off the TV, put down your phone or other devices, forget the to-do list for a little while, and give your spouse loving affirmation through eye contact and touch.

5. Listen generously

Your mate needs the gift of your time and attention. It's hard to take time out of our busy lives to generously give our energy to listening when we have so much to do every day, but communicating openly is key to a healthy marriage. When you listen generously, your mate will feel secure in coming to you with their concerns, hopes, and fears.

"The first duty of love is to listen." ~Paul Tillich

6

Be willing to understand.

Being willing to listen is only half of learning the language of love. The other half is understanding what you hear.

And that means being open to a different perspective, even an opposite view.

At first that sounded like I needed to give up what I believed, to forever bow down on the way I saw things.

Not the case. It meant I needed to learn to see that there could also be an alternative, equally valid viewpoint.

Understanding in love goes beyond being aware and appreciative of the other person's stance and beliefs. It takes consciously embracing that you're one of two, and both your perspectives have a place. Love is big enough to handle different opinions and philosophies.

So the other person grew up in a different culture, for example. That works for them and the millions of people brought up the same. There must be something in it. Love means appreciating that. Although I went to a little school, I'm a country Bunkin in my conversation. My beautiful India is a Northerner. Our dialogue is hilarious sometimes. Especially, when I talking about country clichés. I have to make sure that I'm not too sensitive when she questions my statements.

I learned that speaking your mind doesn't have to be rude or inflammatory, no matter how directly you say it. In some cultures it's rude not to! And yet I'd been programed to never disagree or say the 'wrong thing' and instead to give the accepted, acquiescent response. Love taught me there's another way—that it's more important to be honest and truly understand each other than to simple appease each other.

11 Ways to be More Understanding in a Relationship

There's a reason why understanding is one of the top qualities of a good partner in a romantic relationship. Aside from the fact that this trait allows your partner to be whom they want to be without the fear of being judged, it lets you see things from other people's perspective.

If you're still struggling to know how to be a more understanding mate in a relationship, this book will help you recognize, appreciate and practice this very important characteristic.

Here are ways to be more understanding in a relationship.

1. Take time to get to know your mate better.

The challenge of trying to understand another person lies in one's inability to actually see them not just as a partner but also as a human being capable of different feelings and emotions. It's impossible to truly learn how to understand someone if you don't know them: their strengths, their joys, their fears, and also their imperfections.

As a partner, you have to take your time to get to know your partner better. It might take months or years but it will all be worth it, especially if you want your relationship to last.

2. Be aware of your own feelings and motivations.

Learning how to understand another person can be difficult if you don't even understand yourself. How well do you know yourself? What are the things that make you happy, sad or angry? How do these feelings motivate you? How do they help you make decisions? If you know the answers to these questions about yourself, then it can be easy for you to look at your partner and understand their own struggle.

3.Never impose your own ideals and beliefs.

No matter how much you think that you are better than your partner in terms of experience, maturity or even in intellect, never impose your own ideals and beliefs. Doing so will only leave you blind and unaware of how they truly feel.

If you want to be an understanding partner in a relationship, you should realize that respecting your partner's own convictions and accepting their own beliefs as a part of who they are, are necessary if you want to keep your bond stronger.

4. Allow your partner to live a life outside of your relationship.

Being an understanding partner means recognizing that your relationship is not the center of the universe – and it goes the same with your significant other. In other words, don't force your partner to make your relationship their number one priority – and this includes giving them the freedom to just live and have fun, even if you're not around.

5. Respect your partner's needs as a social being.

Let your partner go out with their friends or spend time with their family. Let them travel solo and live their life to the fullest even in your absence.

Most importantly, let them pursue that personal goal and encourage them to go out into the world and reach their greatest dreams.

6. Remember that you are not always right.

In relation to the previous section, being an understanding partner means listening to what the other person has to say. You are not always right and most of the time, trying to prove that your views, ideas, and judgment are more acceptable can hurt your partner more and can even lead to an argument instead of a resolution.

7. Learn how to compromise.

If you want to be an understanding partner, you have to focus on finding a common ground, on choosing to agree to disagree, instead of pointing out over and over again that you're always right. Remember, your partner is not the enemy and both of you are fighting the same fight.

8. Give your partner time to explain before reacting.

When you think that your partner did something that made you feel angry, upset or disappointed, give them a chance to explain. Hear their side of the story and don't be quick on your judgment.

Sometimes, people in a relationship tend to choose anger and react damaging emotional outbursts before actually talking to their partner.

9. Understand your partner's intentions and motivations.

Learning how to be understanding especially when your partner did something wrong perhaps is the most challenging thing to do, especially if you feel hurt and betrayed. However, you have to find the strength and the love to listen, with full sincerity. Most importantly, you have to have faith in your significant other and give them the chance to understand their intentions and what motivated them to do so.

10. Always choose kindness over anger.

In connection to the previous sections, if there are instances in which you find your partner to be at fault, you have to always choose to be kind than to let anger make things worse. Anger will never solve anything especially if your significant other has done something that could potentially end your relationship.

Anger can be a normal response to an event or an action that hurt you, but it's the wrong direction especially if you want to fix a dying relationship. To be more understanding means to choose to be kind and gentle, letting you heal together while trying to make it work.

11. Help your partner learn from their mistakes.

Being understanding is one of the ways to fix an almost broken relationship. It will help you heal and understand that even if your partner made mistakes, they deserve that second chance to prove herself/himself once again.

In this process, you have to do your part in the relationship by helping your mate to learn from their mistakes. You have to be patient and understanding enough to give it another go. Most importantly, try to focus on their effort rather than the mistakes that they made.

"One of the most beautiful qualities of true friendship is to understand and to be understood." ~Lucius Annaeus Seneca

7

Be willing to accept

Love doesn't have a complicated vocabulary. All it wants to hear is "That's okay. I love you for who you are." Accepting the other person for who they are, however, doesn't guarantee love will flourish in a relationship. For that to have a chance of happening, you have to accept yourself for who you are as well.

To let love in, you need to believe you're worthy of love, that you truly are enough for another's heart to fall for.

You need to embrace your human-ness, your less than polished edges, and all your quirks—and theirs, too, in equal measure.

I had to learn that I didn't need to be perfect. And I never could be. That I needed help sometimes. And doing my best was plenty. I had and have many flaws.

I had to accept that about the other person too. I had to step back and see that no matter how large the mess or miscommunication, they'd gone into the situation dripping with good intentions and love.

Accept that in a relationship you're one of two wonderful, separate, yet intertwined individuals.

You can be the amazing you that you are, and they can be their wonderful self too.

Love in fact, does not conquer all. It's a common misconception that if you love someone, everything else will work itself out, but love alone is not enough.

Acceptance is what will get you through to the other side. Acceptance doesn't mean resignation; it means understanding that something is what it is and that you can choose it for exactly what it is. Because when you do choose it for what it is and what it isn't, it brings something entirely new into your world.

Once there is acceptance, you bring peace and change to your energy, and from there anything you create with the person you love is possible.

That's not to say that you must accept everything in your relationship. You shouldn't accept any abuse, physically or emotionally, and you must establish your deal-breakers along with making sure you are compatible, have similar core values and a vision for your future.

However, there are things you must accept in the one you love and in your relationship in order to bring peace into your life.

Here are 20 things you must accept for your relationship to succeed:

1. Accept the things you cannot change.

2. Accept that you cannot fix your partner.

3. Accept that your partner is not perfect.

4. Accept that not everyone will behave as you do.

5. Accept that just because they don't behave like you, it doesn't make them wrong.

6. Accept their flaws.

7. Accept love as they are able to give it to you.

8. Accept that you love them.

9. Accept that we all experience things (including love) differently.

10. Accept that sometimes they can be a bit of a mess.

11. Accept the mess in the sink.

12. Accept that they are human and will make mistakes.

13. Accept their apology.

14. Accept your differences.

15. Accept that everyone has a past.

16. Accept that they cannot read your mind.

17. Accept that they can't live up to an expectation you don't communicate.

18. Accept that you are not always right.

19. Accept that there will be good and bad times.

20. Accept them.

"The greatest gift you can give to others is the gift of unconditional love and acceptance." ~Brian Tracy

8

Be willing to support

It's hard to put the other person first when your own emotions are raging.

Support starts with looking out for signs the other one is struggling. It means putting your own battles on hold for a while.

I learned how to look beyond my thoughts and problems and truly be there for the other person, thank goodness. And our love deepens every time we do.

To begin with, it's important to remember that our mates are individuals. They have their own desires, hopes, visions and dreams. And while you're likely to partner up with someone who holds similar beliefs about the world, no one is ever going to want everything that you want, too.

Unfortunately, this scares us. We're scared that our partners' dreams might take them away from us, so we may not support them in fulfilling them. What we don't realize is the opposite is actually true: supporting the happiness of your partner encourages them to bring their happiness back to you.

Think about it. How does your relationship feel when your mate is shining; when they're happy, free, and doing what they love? If you're internally secure enough, I imagine it feels great! Most of us love seeing our loved ones shine! We also feel the benefit of it – when we're happy, we share the love.

When someone holds us back, we get resentful. Not a single person on this planet enjoys feeling controlled or stifled. It's completely against our nature; it makes us want to run away.

Support is always the way to go if you want your relationship to thrive. So, how do you do it?

Well, for starters, you have to know what it means to be genuinely supportive. True support is about encouraging someone's growth as a human being. Support doesn't mean we encourage people to do whatever they want, just because they want it.

For example, supporting an alcoholic in their destructive drinking pattern is not being supportive in the name of love. It's enabling. But supporting your partner to take that trip abroad because it's something she's always wanted to do (and she wants to do it alone) is being supportive. See the difference?

Support always encourages growth. And this is why it can be scary. Growth pushes us into the unknown. But having faith in love is trusting that if you support your partner in becoming the best version of himself or herself, it will support your relationship, too.

"Surround yourself with people who provide you with support and love and remember to give back as much as you can in return." ~Karen Kain

9

Be willing to forgive

Whenever there are two people involved, there are going to be mistakes and misunderstandings. That's a given. But the truth is, they are simply opportunities for love in disguise.

Forgiving says, "That mistake is tiny, our love is huge."

And it says it just the same for what feels like a big mistake too. It says our love can weather this—really, it's strong enough.

And more than that, every time you forgive the other person you'll find the compassion to forgive yourself too.

Forgiveness is one of the most important parts of your relationship.

Forgiving your mate if they've done something to upset you is crucial to the success of your relationship.

When you're feeling disappointed, angry or betrayed, the idea of forgiving someone can feel a little bit like giving in – as if, by letting go of your resentment, you're allowing them to 'get away with it'.

It can be more tempting to hang onto negative emotions – acting distant and frosty as a way of punishing the person who has upset you. It's not unusual to feel this way. Working through these kinds of difficult feelings can take some time. But forgiveness is a bold step in the right direction. It involves you being able to make a deliberate decision to put your partner's transgressions – or perceived transgressions - behind you, so you can both move forward together.

Why forgive?

We're sure you've heard clichés such as 'not harboring a grudge' or 'being the bigger person'. Well, in theory, it might all seem straightforward, but, as we all know, forgiveness can be tricky.

It involves you allowing yourself to be vulnerable. Forgiving someone means letting go of your anger and letting go of the 'moral high ground'. It can also be difficult as it may involve having to consider how you yourself contributed to the problem. Although it's tempting to imagine ourselves as completely in the right when it comes to disagreements, there are usually two sides to any argument.

There's a famous quote that goes: 'Holding onto resentment is like drinking poison and expecting the other person to die.' Forgiveness isn't just about retaining harmony in your relationship; it's also about being kind to yourself. If you're not careful, anger can eat away at you and even affect your attitude towards relationships in the future, making you feel more defensive or untrusting.

Communicating clearly

The first step towards forgiveness is understanding. If your partner has done something to upset you, talk about it. Try to communicate to them in a clear, non-confrontational way about how you're feeling. Explain what it is that upset you and why it upset you in the way that it did.

During the conversation, you find it useful to use 'I' phrases ('I feel', 'I would like') rather than 'you' phrases ('you always', 'you don't'). This way, you're taking responsibility for your own feelings and your partner won't feel like you're attacking them. And when it's your mate's turn to talk, listen to what they have to say and try to understand their perspective too.

Mending lost trust can take some time. That's perfectly normal. You can't necessarily expect forgiveness to occur immediately. The important thing is that you take the first steps towards understanding and appreciating how each other feels.

Forgiveness is a skill. Try to learn to build it into your relationship on a day to day basis. By learning to let go of the little things, you'll be able to avoid the kinds of petty conflicts that, over time, can begin to erode away at a relationship.

That doesn't mean simply letting your mate walk all over you. It can, in many cases, mean letting them know that they've upset you, but not dwelling on the issue for long. But it does mean, when appropriate, deciding to not make mountains out of molehills. Every relationship requires a bit of give and take. Learning to forgive can make that whole process a lot easier.

"The reality is people mess up. Don't let one mistake ruin a beautiful thing." ~Unknown

10

Be Willing To Pray For Your Mate

You'll never love your mate more than when you pray for them. Humbling yourself before an all-powerful God an asking Him to do what only He can do in them. That's a level of intimacy beyond anything the world has to offer. Praying for your mate makes you realize how much of a treasure he or she is, the mate that God gave you. You are pouring yourself into their complete physical, emotional and spiritual well-being. From day one, India and I have prayed Together as well as separate. Pray for each other's Growing Need for God, Building Love for one another, Shielding each other from Spiritual Attack and Protecting each other's Joy.

Based on research by John Upchurch, here are some examples of these prayers:

GIVE US A GROWING NEED FOR YOU

Father, you supply all our needs according to Your riches in Christ. I'm amazed that you care about us enough to meet our daily concerns and to notice every detail of our lives. Even the hairs of our heads are numbered because you take care of your children (Philippians 4:19; Matthew 7:11, 10:30).

We confess that we sometimes think of ourselves as being the one who takes care of the other. Forgive us for taking to ourselves what truly belongs to you. Our help comes from You. If we totally depend on each other, we will disappoint each other, but You never fail. You are always faithful and always enough. Help us to know that You are all we need (Psalm 121:2; Lamentations 3:2; Isaiah 58:11; John 12:8-9). If we are tempted to look for comfort in anything else, may we instead realize how the power of Your Holy Spirit allow us to overflow with hope and peace. Nothing on this earth compares to the greatness of knowing You (Romans 15:13; Philippians 3:8).

BUILD OUR LOVE

Father, You loved us first...so much that You sent your Son to take our place. How incredible it is to think that while we were sinners, Christ died for us. Nothing we do could ever compare to the riches of Your grace (1 John 4;19; Romans 5:8; Ephesians 2:7)

Help us to grow first in our love for You. My we be increasingly in awe of Your power, beauty and grace. May we know more each day about the depth and width of Your love and respond with increasing love of our own (Psalm 27:4; Ephesians 3:18).

Help us to love each other through all of our failures while we learn to love each other as Christ loves the church. May we see each other as You see us and may we enjoy fulfilling each other's desires in our marriage (Ephesians 5:25; 1 Corinthians 7:2-4).

Please give us a growing love for each other in all that we do. Show us how to be Christ's Ambassadors in the world and to be a couple defined by love so that others may glorify You. Because of that love, may we share the gospel with everyone (2 Corinthians 5:20; Matthew 5:16; 1 Thessalonians 2:8).

SHIELDING EACH OTHR FROM SPIRITUAL ATTACK

You, God, are a shield around us. You protect us from the enemy who seeks to destroy, and you will not let us be put to shame. Your arm is mighty, and Your Word is powerful (Psalm 3:3, 12:7, 25:20; Exodus 15:9; Luke 1:51; Hebrews 1:3).

When the enemy attacks us, let our faith in You protect us so that we may stand our ground. Bring your Word to our mind so that we say turn aside his assaults and fight the good fight. Help us to remember that You give us the victory through Christ (Ephesians 6:10-18; 1 Timothy 6:12; 1 Corinthians 15:57).

You have conquered and disarmed the spiritual powers and everything is in complete submission to You. Because of the cross, we are a new creation and nothing can separate us from Your amazing, unfailing love (Colossians 2:15; 1 Peter 3:22; 2 Corinthians 5:17; Romans 8:38-39).

The enemy is defeated. You have crushed his head (Genesis 3:15).

PROTECTING EACH OTHERS JOY

Thank you, Father for the gift my mate. You are the giver of all good and perfect blessings and we are amazed how You show Your love through both of us. Please help us to cherish such an amazing gift (James 1:17). Each day, circumstances and frustrations can easily steal the joy from us. Please keep us from letting these challenges tur our focus from You, the author of our faith. Give us the joy that Jesus had as He accomplished the Father's will on earth. May we consider each other's struggles as a reason to find hope in You (Hebrews 12:2-3; James 1:2-3).

When we feel tired, Lord, renew our strength. Surround us with friends who love You and will bear our burdens. Give us reason to feel refreshed by their encouragement (Isaiah 40:31; Galatians 6:2; Philemon 1:7).

May we know that the joy of the Lord is the source of our strength. Protect us from growing tired of doing what You've called us to do each day (Nehemiah 8:10; Galatians 6:9).

11

To India My Engagement Message

To India

To the girl that I saw singing on her church's praise team. You should know that I watched just to see you. Since I had never heard your voice, I listened trying to figure out which voice was yours.

I tried inquiring but my inquiries were left unanswered. So, reluctantly, I just continued to watch from a distance. Until finally it happened. A response on Facebook messenger. You spoke of going to the movies alone.

It wasn't like the R&B group Shai saying, "Hello and you said hi." It was just me on the other end of a keyboard wishing I could have gone with you. (Typing really slow)

I eventually found out that you were skeptical about me. You had your reasons but I still had hope because of what God had promised.

Then the late night discussions began on messenger. I looked forward every night to hearing your concerns and even feeling your pain. I know you got frustrated from time to time because I typed slow. However, I always offered to call, if you would just give me your number. At that time, you never did give me your number. You just messaged me like my fingers were AT&T.

April 5, 2019, God gave a breakthrough. After not being able to keep up on messenger, I asked you out to meet. To my surprise, you agreed. The woman whose voice I'd never heard, was going to be physically in my presence.

I was so excited that I broke all my rules and met you at Red Lobster, instead of Waffle house. Finally, the voice, in the words of the group Shai, I said Hello and you said Hi! At this point, life was good.

Then God revealed to me my mission. It was to love you without reservations. To be a living example of God's Grace and Mercy. To restore you and build you up was the task at hand. At this point not to be taken by your physical beauty but help heal a hurting Queen. It was then that I realized that I was face to face with my wife.

April 5, 2019, will always be a great day in my life. It was that day I accepted the challenge to love you UNCONDITIONALLY.

As we continue to pray together every day, I believe God is going to meet our every need. I look forward to the journey. Love Always, Nard

12

India's Story

One day a friend of mine informed me that this "really nice" gentleman is interested in getting to know me better. She told me how nice he was, gave me a little of his family history and how he had been watching videos of me singing on my praise team on Facebook. I thanked her for the information and that was it. A few days later, she called me again and said that this nice gentleman asked about me again and wanted to know if I was willing to give him my phone number or take his. It was at that point that I explained to her how I was feeling about the last relationship I was in and why I was hesitant. I thanked her for the information and basically that is where it ended. Now here is where I was emotionally at that time....

A few years before I was involved with someone that "I chose" to give my whole heart to. Unfortunately, things did not work out, yet I was still holding on, hoping things would change and go back to the way they were. I felt devastated and felt that I was broken. Little did I know that it was during the time after our breakup that God was working on me. I'd spend many nights awake especially between the hours of 3:00 am to 5:00 am. During that time, I was consistently talking with God, asking for peace, comfort and understanding. I knew God was allowing me to go through what I was going through, I just didn't know why. I know now that God allows us to go through some things so that we are prepared for what he has in store for us.

Fast forward... so me listening to my friend tell me someone is interested in me basically went in one ear and out the other basically because I felt like my heart wasn't ready. Months went by and I saw that this gentleman would make general comments on my Facebook page even though we were not Facebook friends, but he never reached out to me directly. One day, I made a post on Facebook that I was going to try going to the movies alone and see how that would work out (being funny of course). This gentleman made a comment asking me what movie I saw and what were my thoughts about it. Ironically, the movie was titled "What Men Want" so it obviously gave us the opportunity to have some general dialogue although nothing personal. He stated that he had not seen the movie personally but based on our conversation, he was interested in seeing it and he would give me his view when he did. Months went by and we were back to him just commenting here and there on my Facebook page and liking the videos of our praise team singing.

About 2-3 months later, I received a message from my mysterious Facebook friend, telling me that he finally had the opportunity to see the movie and wanted to share with me his thoughts. Our conversations started out talking about the movie but eventually turned into conversations about life in general. Many of these conversations were broken up because he knew I didn't sleep well so he would sometimes start conversations at 3 am and I assume fall asleep in the middle of them. Many times, during our conversations he offered me his number and told me I could call whenever I wanted to. Again, due to my personal issues, I never did because I felt I wasn't ready. This went on for weeks and finally one day, April 5, 2019, he asked me if I would be willing to meet him for dinner. I had reservations, but something said...JUST GO! It's dinner not marriage! Hesitantly I said yes, and we met at a local restaurant.

Because we never talked on the phone, I was nervous about meeting him, but I figured it was daytime, we were in a public place and it was time to step out on faith and do something different. I came inside the restaurant and he came up to me an introduced himself. We shook hands and gave each other "the church hug" and waited to be seated. I felt a little awkward, but he was very nice and made me feel comfortable. We were seated and did the usual "it's finally nice to meet you and put a face to the texts" conversation. He thanked me for finally giving him a chance to talk to me especially face to face because he really didn't expect me to say yes. I told him how I finally decided to just step out on faith and go have some fun...no strings attached. I had no idea what would come next.

After a few general conversations we once again started discussing some of our conversations we had while texting. He had a way of making me feel comfortable to talk to, so I felt the need to share with him why I was hesitant to talk with him on the phone. I told him how I was still dealing with feelings for my ex even though it had been over 2 years since our separation. He patiently listened and before I knew it, I found myself crying and sharing with him my insecurities. It almost felt like a counseling session but unplanned. He eventually tried to make light of the conversation by making a joke that everyone in the restaurant thinks he is breaking up with me. We laughed a little and surprisingly I felt as if a giant weight was lifted off from me. He asked me if he could pray for me, so we held hands in that restaurant and he did just that. I am sure everyone was watching but I felt like there was no one there but us.

For the next several weeks we talked a lot on the phone, had dinner a few times and he even invited me to his family's house for a holiday get together just to get me out of the house. Although I was told that he was interested in me, he never mentioned wanting to have a personal relationship with me during this time. He mostly listened and asked questions that made me think and reflect on my life. He offered spiritual guidance as well when needed and he never stopped praying with me. We have prayed together every day since our first encounter at the restaurant.

One day he finally told me that he was still interested in me and wanted to pursue a relationship with me but only if I was ready. I almost forgot he was interested in me especially since he so patiently listened to me talk about my feelings for someone else. Anyway, we discussed what things we both wanted in a relationship with GOD being the center for both of us and what "love" meant to each of us. Then he shared with me that he loved me and that he loved me the first day he saw me in the restaurant. I honestly cannot tell you at what point I loved him, I just did! God showed me this was my husband, the man I asked him to send me for years. I know now that God was preparing me for him in all that I have gone through in my previous relationships. I needed to go through everything I had gone through so that I could appreciate him once he found me. Yes, he found me!

I truly feel that my failures at relationships have always been because I allowed my feelings to get involved and control my decisions. As women, once we like a man and our feelings get involved, we find ourselves doing almost anything to try to please that man in hopes that he will feel like we feel. Many times, we forget that men are not wired the way we are and most of them do not make decisions based on "feelings." They may be interested in us, but it's usually physical, at least at first.

I believe as women, we need to allow the blueprint that God set for us to follow. God made Adam and then he made Eve to be his "helpmate."

In the Bible, God commanded man to love his wife as Christ loved the church (Eph 5:25). God did not command the woman to love the man nowhere in the Bible because he by design, if the man followed his command, the woman would love him automatically. Why? Because as women we want to be cared for, protected and loved. If the man is doing this, we will fall in love with him. This is what happened with me. This gentleman cared about my feelings, he listens to me, he makes me feel safe and cared for. I feel he always has my best interest at heart and is genuinely concerned for my spiritual well-being. I thank God for allowing me the opportunity to receive my Boaz!

About The Authors

Henry Bernard Miller is the Director of Chaplaincy Services at Georgia Diagnostic and Classification Prison. He also serves as Associational Strategist for Statewide Association of Baptist Assemblies.. He conducts workshops and Training sessions all over the Nation. He has a grown son and daughter. Both are married. He also has two grandsons.

India Miller is a US Army Veteran, a Registered Nurse Manager, a mother of three grown daughters as well as a grandmother to two beautiful granddaughters. She also serves as Chaplain.

You may contact them at pastorhbm@yahoo.com., indiahudsonrn@gmail.com chaplain1211@gmail.com

Henry Bernard Miller (FB)

Workshops Available:

Every Believer is a Witness

Knowing Those That Labor With You (Personalities

Building Small Groups That Grow Your Church

Leadership 101 (Leaders Set The Pace)

Pathway Too Biblical Recovery. Let's Get Healed

How to Know your Mate by Knowing Yourself.

Personal and Pre-Marital Counseling

Made in the USA
Columbia, SC
28 February 2025

54538255R00033